written by
Alessandra Sgubini

Principles of Problem Solving for Kids

Stuck In Conflicts? Handy Roadmap To Act & Think As Problem Solvers!

Printed in the United States of America
ISBN 978-0-578-60681-1

Acknowledgements

"A vision without an execution is an illusion."

Execute any idea, any vision or even a dream is not easy.

To make sure an idea will become a reality requires strength and faith that the idea will become real. To realize an idea requires a lot of work and talented people with different skills to work as a team toward the same goal.

I want to thank the valuable individuals for their amazing talents and skills. They believed, dreamed and kept working with me even when all seemed very complicated in spite of outsiders telling us that the idea was impossible.

I give my special thanks to Ben Graily, who shared with me his wisdom and humor; to Daniel Aiers, a very capable illustrator who was able to design my ideas; to Jeffrey Schaffer for his friendship and patience in editing and re-editing the stories; to Kozakura who designed the layout of the book in such creative way and finally to Irving Partida who worked with me in locating the artists and managed the deadlines.

Introduction

Have you ever wondered: "*Why do people, more than ever, get into conflicts all the time?*"

I spent the last 20 years of my professional life dealing with people involved in all kinds of conflicts (professional and personal) from the most complicated to the easiest, and I believe I have the answer to "*why do the majority of people get in trouble?*"

My answer is: "*The majority of people don't have the skills, mind and tool sets to handle properly, effectively and productively the interactions with others especially when conflicts or problems arise. People don't like to be responsible for their own actions or for what they say. They prefer to blame others for their problems and prefer to rely on a third party to get them out of trouble instead of working directly toward the right solution for them.*"

This book is made up of 9 differents funny kid's stories. Each story is based on problem solving principles and the stories are made for the younger generation to be familiar with concepts that will make them successful adults.

In today's techno Era where more and more people communicate behind a screen, a phone, a computer etc. without any personal connection. It's now time to teach the importance of individuals' ability to open a dialogue with others face to face.

I firmly believe, from a young age, each individual have the skills to manage effectively any interaction and prevent conflicts. People just need to be aware of the tools we all have and learn how to use them effectively.

Through the 9 funny adventures of the book experienced by the two main characters, Molly and Jack, the reader learns how important are the skills, the attitude and the abilities of the Problem Solvers and the Principles of Problem-Solving process.

Molly and Jack with the help of Sally, the oldest girl, at the end of the adventures are able to build a roadmap to show what they learned and what to do to overcome conflicts effectively, productively and efficiently when problems arise.

They call it "**The Problem-Solving Roadmap**".

The Roadmap can be used by everyone regardless of their age. It allows one to understand concepts such as communication, verbal and non-verbal language, perception of reality, conflicts, methods to resolve them such as mediation, the concept of "the" right solution and how important it is the "after" conflicts. Through the Roadmap is possible to focus on searching what might be the right solution for the parties and actively participate to reach the solution. The Problem-Solving Roadmap allows the users to become a Problem Solver and have a process to follow.

The final goal is to build self-confidence and awareness of skills, tools, and abilities that everyone has, but no one uses them correctly to build a happy life without conflicts. If we are able to teach the young generation to understand that it is not always about us, and to know that people perceive reality in a different ways and believe there is always a possibility to overcome conflicts, we will see a new generation of adults.

Table of Contents

Penny The Giraffe,
Leo The Hippo And Sam The Big Tree
"We Are All Different"

1

Penny The Giraffe, Leo The Hippo And Sam The Big Tree "We Are All Different"

"Hi, my name is Molly and the funny looking guy next to me is Jack, my best friend."

"People are always asking us: Why are you always happy and playful? Actually, I don't know the answer maybe because we are conflict free." Molly says

We are friends since we were born, and we share the same passion, the love for the ocean. Both of us love to swim and surf in the big waves. We want to be lifeguards when we grow up. We wake up early every day to go surfing before school and we study hard to be able to go to swim practice in the afternoon. Other kids cannot understand why we do it all and even more they don't understand why we are always smiling, happy and have time to do it all, like schools, friends, swimming and surfing.

More often than not Jack and I can communicate without words just watching each other's body language. Watching and observing the world around us helps us know what the others are thinking without the use of words. For us actions speak louder than words.

"I know it's hard to comprehend how people can communicate without words so let me tell you a story that happened a few weeks ago to us that show perfectly how all of us can communicate without words just acting and using creative thinking".

It was a sunny and warm day in Southern California.

I guess it's nice to live where is always warm even in the winter.

We always ride our scooters back home after school.

That particular day we were super excited to get back home and tell our parents we both got accepted to the swim and surf teams of the junior lifeguard.

We are always taking the same street to go back home because there are some down hills that are super fun to jump with the scooters. We know the street better than our own backyards.

Suddenly, Jack who was a little ahead of me calls me: *"Molly, come over here, there is a strange Puddle of water"* he says.

When I got there, it was true, a very blue and clear puddle of water not bigger than 3-feet wide was reflecting images that we could not understand where they came from.

Before, I know it Jack rides his scooter into the puddle of water and "POOF" disappeared.

Even though I was so scared, I always follow him in his crazy actions.

I ride my scooter into the puddle of water as well and "POOF".

15

Before we could realize what was going on,
we found ourselves in this amazing park with
the most beautiful trees, flowers and creeks.
The sky is so blue that it seems the color of the
ocean where we train every day.

16

Jack looks at me and says: "Molly it seems we are in another world! Where are we? Are you happy I brought you here?"

"I want to hit you, but I must admit it's awesome here." Molly replies

We are near a giant tree the most beautiful tree we have ever seen.

We got up from the ground and left our scooters near the big tree.

We look in the horizon to understand where we are, and we see a beautiful lake down the hill and around the lake there are hundreds of animals having a big party. Everyone is having a great time dancing and singing.

Even though we are curious and amazed by what was happening and what we were seeing, we are super scared to been seen by the animals, so we hide behind the big tree.

When suddenly we heard:

"Welcome kids to our world. I am Sam the Big Tree. Please don't be scared. The animals around the lake are super friendly and welcome everyone to be a part of us. Unfortunately, they don't speak your language, so they won't know the meaning of the words that you are going to say to them. They, probably, will get scared when they will see you. They never saw kids before from the outside world. Please, do not be scared of them and here some words that can help you when you start to talk to them to create the bond".

Eboo Eboo means - Hi

Baash, Baash means - friends

Kuky means - we are kids from the outside world.

We got so scared hearing the giant tree talk that before we knew it we were running breathless down the hill and in less than a minute we are around the lake with all the animals.

As soon as the animals see us, they stopped dancing and singing and started screaming being terrified. Hearing them screaming we start to scream as well. The noise being so loud that our heads started spinning and we felt like we were going to pass out.

At one-point, Penny the giraffe said: "*quiet everyone I think those are KIDS from the outside world the ones that Sam the Big tree always used to talk about.*"

"*OHHHHHH* "all the animals say.

Jack and I at this point were really terrified. I whisper into Jack's ear:

"*Jack do you remember what the big tree said before we got scared and ran away. He tried to say something to us. I cannot remember.*"

Jack at this point has his mouth open and he seems in a state of trance.

"*Jack, Jack can you come back to me in the present moment and listen to me, do you remember what the big tree tried to tell us when he talked?*"

Jack after few minutes starts saying crazy words:

"*Eboo Eboo, Baash Baash,, Kuky*"

I am thinking "*OHH My God he is going out of his mind ....*"

Penny the Giraffe heard Jack saying these words and came up to us and said the same exact words.

"*OHHHH* "Jack and I are amazed and in a state of shock, we cannot almost breathe.

We realized the big Tree had tried to teach something to us, but we were not listening because we were too scared.

"*Jack, we need to breath and calm down otherwise we really cannot resolve this situation and that means we will never get back home. We cannot get in panic mood and be scared because those emotions won't make us think straight.*"

So now together we say: "*one, two, three breathe*" Molly says.

While we are breathing, I am smiling, Jack is always making me smile and laugh also in difficult situations like this one. This time he says:

"*Molly, we look like our moms when they do yoga and we hate yoga.*"

Molly says: "*Jack please can you be serious for once. This is not the right time to be funny and make me laugh we are in trouble and in a very difficult situation. If you didn't realize it we are in a different world where trees talk, animals speak a language we don't have a clue what their words mean, and we don't know how to get back home.*"

Jack looks at Molly and says: "*keep breathing one, two, three. Don't worry everything will be ok*".

While we were breathing and counting one, two, three Leo the Hippo comes close to Penny the giraffe, and at this point she is really close to us.

Penny the giraffe and Leo the Hippo start to mirror what we are doing breathing and smiling. The 4 of us are doing the same thing and now we really seem to be in our mom's yoga class.

In the distance the rest of the animals stopped to scream and start walking toward us to see what we were doing.

Few minutes later Jack says: *"I guess the giraffe and hippo like us. Even though we don't understand what they are saying, and they don't understand what we are saying we are doing the same thing. I guess this is a good thing."*

"Molly, we should introduce ourselves and say that even though we are different, look strange and we are outsiders we are friends." Jack says, *"Without their help we don't know how to get back home."*

Molly says: *I don't' know how to tell them that. We don't speak the same language so how can we communicate with them?"*

Jack thought for a little bit and after says: *"We should mirror what they did before they saw us. The last thing we saw was the dancing and singing around the lake, so let's start to dance."*

Molly says:" Jack you don't know how to dance even though you think you do, you don't."

Molly is thinking in her head: "The way Jack's dance is putting his hands in the air and moves the feet one at the time up in the air. Let's hope the animals are not getting scared by him moving in a very unique way."

Jack starts to dance, and Molly follows him and few minutes later all the animals mirror them.

Penny says to Leo: "I like how the boy moves I should copy what he is doing." Leo says: "The boy seems crazy, but he is fun to watch".

We danced for hours until Jack says "let me rest for few minutes I am really tired"

Everyone becomes exhausted and fall asleep.

Leo the Hippo is always the first to wake up in the park and saw Molly and Jack sleeping next to Penny.

Jack wakes up and wakes Molly up.

"*Molly, we need to make Penny the giraffe understand that we need her help to go back home. How can we make them understand us? We need their help. At this point the animals are our only friends who can helps us. They are the only ones to help us to figure out how to go back home.*"

We try to communicate with Penny and Leo in our language, but they could not understand. So, Leo and Penny started to be very frustrated, and we are getting frustrated as well because they could not understand us.

When suddenly we see Leo communicate with Penny in their language, Leo says to Penny: "*Penny do you remember Sam the big tree he is so wise and old that probably he knows what the kids are trying to say. Let's bring them to him*"

"*We didn't know what they said to each other, but we saw Leo and Penny start to walk up the hill quietly and calm.*" Molly says

Molly says to Jack: "*Let's mirror what they do, like they mirror us before. We should follow them and start walking.*"

So, Jack and Molly follow them.

We are walking up the hill that we came down from and recognized the trees, flowers and creeks. Quietly, without saying a word, we follow Leo and Penny, until we got in front of the big tree.

"Ohhhh Molly this is the big tree that we saw when we got here that talked to us." Jack says: "Look, there are our scooters".

The big tree seems sleepy and quite like as a tree should look like.

Penny and Leo stop in front of the Big Tree and start to say something in their language. We could not understand a thing and to us it seemed like: "MAAAAAA HAHHAN MAAAA"

The big tree didn't' make any noise or moves.

After a short time, Penny and Leo start to play hide and seek and we could not help, and we start to play with them forgetting why we were there.

Until we heard "AUCH!!" so loud with a very scary sound (it's seems like when Mr. Johnson last year came over the house and fell off the chair in our living room on his back")

The voice starts to say:" Hi Penny and Leo, I see that you found your new friends. Hi Kids, I am Sam the Big Tree of the park, do you remember? I met you before. Sorry, if I scared you, but Jack just stepped on my root and hurts.

Jack says: "OHH, I am so, so sorry Sam the Big Tree."

Sam replies: "Penny and Leo told me that you would like my help and you have a question for me, but they don't understand what you are saying."

Molly says: "Yes, Sam we would like your help to figure out how we can get back home even though we like it here very much we are missing our home and families."

Sam replies to them: "Sure, I understand. The only way you can get back home is that you are going to Ms. Berry the most beautiful tree in the park, and she will show how to get back home. When you get in front of Ms. Berry tree knock on the trunk and when she opens, she will ask a question this is the only way to get back home."

"See kids, when you jump in the puddle of water you come into our world. Only special people can visit us and when you are so lucky to be coming in our world you need to bring back to your world the lesson you learned in the journey."

Molly asks: *Which question?*

Sam replies: *"She will ask you what you learned from this journey to be sure that when you are back home you can share with others what you learned and experienced."*

Jack and Molly thought for a while and Molly says: *"We are ready!"*

Sam the big tree says: *"Penny and Leo, can you bring the kids to Ms. Berry tree."*

28

"We got to Ms. Berry the beautiful tree and knocked." Molly says.

Ms. Berry opens the door and asks the question, as Sam The Big tree said.

Jack starts to talk first, as always, and says:

"We learned that being different is good and the animals like how I danced. I think it is boring to be all the same, dress the same, talk in the same way.

I don't think we should be scared when we see things, we are not familiar with, but instead we need to take time to understand who is in front of us and who they are. Often things are not what they seem. And finally, we need to find the way to communicate in a way the others will understand. More often than not words are not so important as much as what we do."

Molly jumps in the conversation and says:

"Well, I don't think Jack knows how to dance but he is right, we are all different and all of us have something in common. All love to dance and singing so this is what we have in common and from there we start to create a bond and communicate.

It doesn't matter how different we are, which language we speak and how we look like because all of us like to laugh and be happy. All of us need to have the friends that helps us in the hard time to overcome the difficult situations. We need to build a circle of friends that will help us to reach what is good for us.

Ms. Berry the beautiful tree says: "WOW! Very good kids. It seems you learned the lesson of this journey, now Jeffrey the Mouse will take you to the red door. When you get there, you will open it and you will get home to your family.

Jack and Molly found themselves in their homes, in their bedrooms with their scooters. Few minutes later their respective mothers called them: "*Dinner is ready.*"

The Special Glasses
"The Perception Of Reality"

2

The Special Glasses
"The Perception Of Reality"

Molly wakes up to get ready to go to school and before going downstairs to have breakfast she stops by Jason's room to wake him up.

Jason is 6 years old and he is Molly's brother. He is funny and smart. Since he was 4 years old, he was able to do Molly's homework.

"*Jason, wake up! Today will be your first school day*". Molly says "*Mom, Dad, Jack and I are taking you to school*".

"*Is everyone ready?*" Molly asked. "*Jack is waiting for us*".

Jack is in the doorway waiting for Molly's family and as soon as he sees them, he runs toward them while they pull into driveway.

"*Ready Jason*" Jack says, "*It's going to be so cool the first day of school. You will meet new friends*".

Jason replies: "*I am a little bit nervous. Maybe the other kids won't like me with my special glasses on*".

"Of course, they will love you" Jack says "and to those who don't, you will smile at them and move on. Remember who you are, what you do and say, and remember as long as you are polite with everyone, play fair and help others in the best of your abilities you will be fine.

Always remember to say: "Hi, please and thank you". You cannot expect to be liked by everyone and vice versa you don't have to like everyone. At the end of the day you just need to like yourself and be yourself. You will always have me and Molly that love you and wear the same glasses".

"Actually", Jack says "let me put on my special glasses."

Molly, Jack, Jason and the parents were wearing special glasses in different colors to be like Jason.

Jason cannot see color of the people's faces. He only sees green faces. He needs to wear special glasses to see all the colors of the world around him, but still he cannot see the color of people's faces.

"Here we are" Jack says, "look how many kids".

"Remember Jason", Molly says "We will see you in few hours when we will come to pick you up and promise me you'll have fun".

"Ok see you at the end of school and I promise you, I will have fun" Jason replies.

Jason enters in the new classroom and it is full of new faces and new kids.

Mr. Robinson, the new teacher, welcomes everyone in and invites them to take a seat. He starts to go through the list of names and calls everyone by their first names.

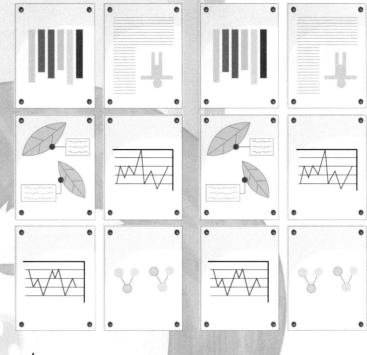

Jason sits near Ali a nice girl with blond curly hair and a big beautiful smile. "*She seems nervous*", Jason is thinking.

"*Hi*" Jason says." *My name is Jason. What is your name?*"

"*Ali*" she says.

Ali after few minutes says to Jason:" *Jason I like your glasses are they special?*"

Jason is afraid to say that the glasses are special but remembers what Jack said in the morning on the way to school and replies:

"Yes, *they are. These glasses help me see the colors of the world, but even with them on I see people's faces green*".

"OHHHH" Ali replies *"so you cannot see that Robert in the back of the class has different color skin, as well as Julia and Patrick"*.

"Yep" Jason says *"for me they are all the same color, all green faces! So, when adults are talking about the color of people skins, I smile because for me they are all green even those that are*

pointing out the differences in people, for me they are green too. I don't see the differences.

"I think it is a good thing that I don't see the differences."

Jason says, "Ali, after school, if you want, I will tell you the backpacks story".

Ali is so curious to hear the story.

The school bell rings, and everyone is going out of school. Jason and Ali are out front waiting for Molly and Jack.

Few minutes pass by and Molly and Jack arrive to pick Jason up.

"Ali," Jason says" *Molly is my sister and Jack is our friend"*.

Ali notices everyone is wearing the same glasses and asks, "you two also are wearing the special glasses?"

"Sure" all of us reply and smile: *"We are like Jason we don't see the differences and we treat people in the same way. It doesn't matter who they are and where they come from the most important thing for us is what they say, how they say it and what they do."*

Ali says to Jason" *you promised me to tell me the story of the backpacks."*

"Ok" Jason says and turns to Molly and says, "can we wait few minutes before going home?"

Molly and Jack say: "Actually, we need to go to swim practice. Do you mind Ali if Jason will tell you the backpacks story tomorrow after school?"

"I understand" Ali replies "Sure no problem. I cannot wait for tomorrow."

The Backpacks Story
"We Are What We Do And What We Say".

3

The Backpacks Story "We Are What We Do And What We Say".

At the end of school day Ali and Jason run out of school.

Molly and Jack are waiting for Jason.

Jason says: "*Molly you promised Ali to stop after school to tell her the backpacks story.*"

Molly says:" *Sure*".

So, the 4 of them sit on the school ground next to the tree with their legs crossed and Jason starts to tell the story.

"Each of us from the youngest kid to the oldest person carry 2 backpacks.

People carry the backpacks all day every day. The backpacks are invisible, and you cannot see them, but they are always there. If you know where to look and what to look for you can see them.

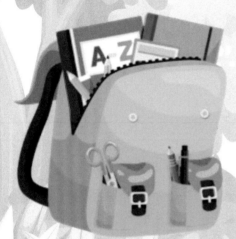

One backpack is bigger, heavier and blue and if you look inside you can find how people are able to talk to others, use the verbal and nonverbal language and able to communicate their thoughts effectively. This backpack controls what they do, how they behave with others and if they have self-esteem or not.

This backpack is difficult to manage and to change. It has many elements inside that are built during a lifetime and based of the events that happened to the person during their lifetime. It's difficult to change and it takes a long time to fill it up.

The second backpack is smaller, lighter and red. If you look inside you can find the daily emotions, feelings, and the daily mood of the person. How people wake up in the morning will affect how they act during the day. The unexpected things that happen daily to the person will as well effects the mood of the person.

Finally, all the duties and responsibilities that each individual has to accomplish daily such as going to school or parents going to work will determine the mood of the person. This backpack is easier to manage and can change every day.

All of us have these 2 backpacks and they determine how we interact with others. In fact, each of us as part of the society, we interact every single day with others from when we wake up to when we go to sleep.

How we handle our two own backpacks and if we are able to see the other's backpacks will determine the success or failure of the interactions.

If we have a positive attitude, we are aware of ourselves, we know what we do and say, and use time wisely we can build a strong and happy life.

Due to these abilities and differences, conflicts will happen and it's a natural part of life, so, there is nothing to be afraid of. They happen because people interact with each other. It's not possible to always agree or see things in the same way. It's also not possible to like everyone or be liked by everyone.

Knowing this, will make people aware how to approach any interaction even the difficult ones in a successful way. They won't get personal and they work effectively to manage their own and other's backpacks.

It's not always about you. It's about who is around you.

Unfortunately, the majority of people don't know about the backpacks, how to interact properly with others and they take everything personal. As a result, they react to what is just different and fight.

They don't take time to think what will be good for them, the consequences of their actions and what the fight will create in their lives.

The ability to look for what is in the backpacks and manage them allows to know how to interact with others.

There are three types of interactions: normal, difficult and the last one is a true conflict.

A good interaction is defined as an interaction between people where the individuals involved deal with each other without any particular challenges and actually bring good into the relationship.

When individuals are able to have a good relationship, they always need to work and put efforts to keep it positive.

Sometimes the interactions from good can turn to be difficult creating difficult situations. A **Difficult situation** is defined as a situation arises when the differences between the individual involved start to show and become more evident. The differences, instead being managed, they create barriers that interrupt the relationship. The difficult interaction can happen due to certain events, behaviors, language used or communication styles.

In this case it's important the individual is able to act sooner than later to address the issues when they arise.

More often than you think the difficult situations are not managed well and conflicts arise.

A **Conflict** is a situation where the differences between the individuals escalated in something bigger than the individuals themselves. Those differences are getting out of control. The different positions, interests, needs and the emotions involved are taking over the thinking process of what is good for the person.

So, when people are getting blinded for their negative emotions such as revenge, resentment and dislike their abilities to be able to make the right decision for themselves become lost. The only thing they are able to do is to react based on principles instead of act on what is good for them.

Problems and conflicts arise everywhere, among different types of parties, in different parts of the world, and for different reasons.

It is a true statement saying, "if conflict is not addressed properly it can escalate leaving serious damages in the individuals' life".

Molly and Jack are amazed by Jason cleverness.

Ali says: "The main goal of all of us is to be aware of our backpacks and manage them effectively and spend time to learn about the backpacks of others."

"This will make the interactions effective and productive".

Molly says: "*Don't be afraid of conflict and when conflict arises act on it to search for the best solution for you.*"

Try to be conflict free.

Being conflict free means that the single individual is more effective, efficient, productive and overall happier.

When an individual is conflict free, he can concentrate on being creative and accomplish what will be good for him and as a final result the whole society will benefit.

Ali was quiet and amazed and says,

"*Can you give me a pair of your special glasses?*"

"*I want to learn how to look in my backpacks and in the backpacks of others to be able to know how to handle the interactions with others effectively. I want to be conflict free.*"

Jo The Shark
"Did You Know?"

4

Jo The Shark
"Did You Know?"

It's another beautiful early morning in Southern California.

Those kind of mornings after a big storm where the ocean looks so calm, peaceful, and the air is fresh and clean.

The sun is not fully out yet but it's coming out slowly behind the hill and the sky is bluer than the ocean.

Jo the Shark wakes up early, as usual, and decided to patrol the Cove. After the storm with big waves, wind and the cold water he wants to make sure everyone is ok in his underwater park called "The Cove". He is always kind and nice to all the habitants of the Cove. He always wants to make sure everyone is doing fine and don't need anything.

Meantime on shore Jack convinced Molly to jump in the water to just swim around the cove to see if they could see anything especially like Silver the seal, Pedro and Bella the turtles and Larry the lobster.

"Molly" says Jack "let's go to see Pedro and Bella the turtles and probably if we are lucky, we will meet Jo the shark. You know you cannot control the ocean."

"Jack please it's not funny I don't want to see any shark and it's too early the sun is not fully out and for sure sharks are out" Molly replies.

As always Jack with his looks and his funny way to make everything fun convinces Molly to go and they jump in the water.

"AHHAHAHH" AHAHHAH" Molly screams while getting in the cold water. "The water is refreshing, and luckily the sun is warm and makes the difference when it heats our backs." Molly says.

Stroke after stroke and kick after kick we arrive at the underwater park and Jack says:

"Come I show you turtle rock. I found it yesterday. There is this big rock in the underwater park shaped as a turtle. You should see it". Jack says.

Jack says to Molly "wait for me here, I will go down and grab Larry"

"What?" Molly replies. "Who is Larry? And where do you go? don't leave me alone, I am scared to be alone and especially I am scared of sharks".

Jack laughs and dives down.

Molly is a little bit anxious and looking around to make sure no sharks are around.

Suddenly, Jack appears next to her with Larry the Lobster in his hand and shows to Molly.

Molly jumped and swam backward and says: "OHHH my Lord, please Jack, leave that poor lobster alone."

Larry is used to Jack and he is playing dead while Jack is showing Larry to Molly

Jack says: "*look when I let Larry go, he will go down super-fast*"

"*For sure*" Molly replies "*probably he was with his family watching TV and you went and bothered everyone. He needs to get back to whatever he was doing.*"

Jack and Molly continue to swim and suddenly, Pedro and Bella the turtles, are swimming gently around the underwater park.

Molly screams:" *Jack look Pedro and Bella are here*".

It is so amazing the Turtles are swimming at the bottom of the ocean and every now and then come up to take a little breath of air and the sun is like a beam of light following them.

When suddenly Molly feels uneasy like someone is watching.

Jo the Shark is behind her.

Molly screams so loud that Jack jumps out of the water wondering what was going on.

"What happened Molly? Why are you screaming like there's no tomorrow?"

"Jack there is a shark around us!" Molly replies

"No worry it's probably Jo the shark, checking if everything around the underwater park is fine after the storm. Molly don't be so afraid. Jo is vegetarian shark". "I am telling you nothing to worry about, he is vegetarian."

Molly faster than light reaches Jack and in less than a second she is over his shoulders and replies: *"Never heard such thing vegetarian sharks. Have you ever seen Shark Week on Discovery Channel? They bite".*

Jack keeps laughing and saying to Molly:

"*Did you know that Jo is even thinking to go vegan*".

Molly replies: "*What is wrong with you! For sure we are the raw meat he is looking for.*"

While Molly is still on Jack's shoulders a soft and warm voice come out of the ocean.

Jo the shark is saying:

"*Hi Jack, how are you today? Do you know you have a person on your shoulder? Who is she?*".

Jack says:"
Hi super Jo, I am doing fantastic! Nice seeing you. How are you after the big storm last night? Is everything and everyone ok in the underwater park?"

"Ohhh, I forgot the crazy girl on my shoulder is Molly. She is my best friend and she is afraid of you".

"AHAHAHAHAHH" Jo starts to laugh "Did you tell her I am vegetarian?"

"Yes, but she didn't believe me" Jack replies.

"Well, tell her not to be scared of me. I am just different and what people are saying about us sharks are not real. I need to go now. I need to check if everything is ok after the storm in the park".

"Before I go can you ask Molly this question: does she know who is at the center of the universe? Jo the shark says.

61

Jack gets puzzled by Jo's question and says:

"I, myself, don't know who is at the center?"

Jo replies:

"*Each one of us are
the center of our own universe, you
are at the center of the universe.
We need to keep in mind that
we perceive reality all different
and therefore to be able to get along with
others we need to understand
in order to know how others
perceive the reality.*"

"*Now I need to go Jack*" Jo says, "*I need to check on everyone and swam away.*"

While he is swimming and patrolling the underwater park, he saw that everyone in the ocean was waking up and the sun was heating up the surface of the ocean. Pedro and Bella, the turtles were taking a walk and having breakfast close to the surface; Larry the lobster with his family were going to visit the grandparents.

Jo the Shark happy and satisfied decided in this warm and calm day to rest and drink a nice iced tea on his favorite beach chair under the big umbrella.

While Jack and Molly got back to shore and get ready to go to school.

The Flying Shoes
"Don't Tell Me What To Do!"

5

The Flying Shoes
"Don't Tell Me What To Do!"

Jack and Molly are super excited. They are getting ready to go to their friend Ben's house for the first time. Ben is the new kid at school. He moved from Italy with his family to Southern California. His father is a diplomat and they travel all over the world representing their country. He has the most amazing stories to tell.

Ben is super smart, funny and sharp. He speaks with his Italian accent that sometimes twist the sound of words. Even if he speaks with an accent, he doesn't think with an accent in fact he is the best in class. At the beginning it was a little hard to understand him but now actually everyone at school says words like Ben does and everyone understands him perfectly.

"It's only a matter of time to get used to what we are not used to" Molly says, *"at the beginning it can be hard but when you getting familiar with new things everything seems easier."*

Jack and Molly are excited because they heard that the apartment where Ben lives with his family is super cool. It's located in downtown in one of those very high-end skyscrapers.

"Actually, Molly and I don't care about the fancy building, we just care about the many techno things they have around the house we can play with." Jack says.

"*Jack are you ready*" shouts Molly from downstairs "*you are worse than I am. It takes a million years for you to get ready*".

"*Ready, ready*" Jack screams from upstairs "*I am coming. I have to put gel in my hair. You never know maybe there are nice girls at the party.*"

"*Seriously*" Molly replies. "*Chop, chop! Move it, we are super late*"

"*We get in the car with Molly's parents. My parents will come directly there with another car*" Jack says.

"*We enter into the lobby and it seems like a 6 star hotel than an apartment building with a door man.*" Molly says.

"*Welcome all, I guess you are the guests of the Gallo Family. They are waiting for you in the penthouse. Let me show where to go.*" Mr. Green the door man says.

"*We get in the super-fast elevator that took all of us to the 45th floor, in less than a minute.*" Jack says. "*When the door opens Ben and his Mom are already waiting for us and welcome us into the apartment.*"

"*WOW*" Jack says, "*I never ever saw a view of downtown from so far up, it seems we are in the sky*".

"The apartment is super nice, big, cozy, full of light with these huge windows. It really seems we are up in the sky" Jack says.

Ben asks all of us to leave our shoes outside the door. He says: "It's our family tradition, since I was little in Italy".

"Perfect I love walking barefoot" Jack says.

Molly looks at Ben and says:" *I am sorry Ben I don't feel comfortable walking barefoot. Do you have flipflop or slippers to lend me?"*

"Sure" Ben replies *"here are bunch of flipflops or slippers for all the people like Molly".*

Jack looks at Molly and says *"Really, you can walk barefoot! Everyone loves to walk barefoot. I guess you are the only one. You are such a princess".*

Molly replies *"leave me alone you know me I just don't do it."*

The tables in the living room are full of Italian food and drinks and the smell in the house is amazing.

"Guests keep coming and in less that 30 minutes we were so many people in the apartments" Jack Says.

"We are having a good time; the adults are talking, some kids are playing videogames, some others are playing board games and others are watching Ben's Mom cooking. My Mom always cooks for everyone" Ben says.

Suddenly, someone rings the bell.

Our friend Billy's father who is close to the door, opens the door with a big smile and says:

"Welcome! Come on in, everyone is in the living room and if you want to learn how to cook Italian food you should go to the kitchen. Ms. Gallo is giving a cooking class"

"I don't want to come in. I am, Mrs. Richards, I live next door. Did you see how many shoes are outside in the hallway?"

"OH WOW" Billy's father says: "let me call Mr. Gallo the owner of the house."

By the time that Ben's father gets to the door, Mrs. Richard starts screaming: "we are in a civilized country and the hallway is not made to be a shoe store."

Ben's father tries to calm her down, but nothing is working.

So, my other friend's Mom steps into the conversation and starts to say: "I don't think shoes are a big deal in the hallway and you need to calm down. You are rude."

At this point Mrs. Richards goes ballistic and starts to scream louder: "probably in your dirty and smelly homes it is not a problem but, in a place, where we share hallways it is a problem. I am not rude".

Ben's father tries to jump in the fight, but he is not very successful because now some of the shoes that were outside are flying inside, *"I am talking more than 100 pair of shoes"* Jack says.

Few shoes fell out of the window and went down onto Sally 's patio. Sally is a young beautiful woman that lives on the 10th floors. Sally saw the shoes falling from the top floors and wonders what is going on upstairs. She decides to go upstairs to check what was happening.

"Hello" Sally says while she opens the door to enter the apartment. As soon as she opens the door a shoe hits her on the head *"OUCH! What is happening here?"*

She sees everyone throw shoes at each other and screaming.

Sally shouts and stands up on a chair. *"Please, please can everyone stop? Someone sooner or later will get hurt"*

A moment of silence and everyone turn toward Sally to look at her.

Mrs. Richard said, *"who are you?"*

"Well, I can ask you the same question" Sally replies and adds *"Now everyone take a deep breath and count to 10"* *"Please can you see that the kids are all scared and are watching you."*

Ben's mom asks nicely to all the guests to move to the patio upstairs, but Molly and Jack stay and hide to see what was going to happen.

Mrs. Richards says: "*There are so many shoes outside in the hallway*". "*I have told this family many times that we don't leave shoes outside the home, but they actually don't care.*"

Mrs. Richards continues: "*At the beginning I told them in a polite way* " *Please do not do it. Since it continued this time, I really get mad and scream to make myself heard.*

I always do things this way. You cannot tell me what to do.

I don't want to change the way I do things. I was nice at first and no one listed to me so now I got mad and here we are. This is how I manage things and it always worked just fine for me."

Perfect" Sally replies, "*I understand this is how you do things and it's good and works for you. However, from what I can see now shoes are flying in the air and down from the window while you are really mad and kids are scared. So, I guess we need to do something different and work something out to resolve this situation.*"

At this point you have 2 options very different from each other.

The first option is to keep fighting and throw shoes out the window and until someone from the street will call the police. The police will come up here, and they will decide for you what to do. After that you both need to call a third party, like lawyers, that will represent you in front a judge to decide who is right and who is wrong. The time from when the third party will take over till the end of the conflict both of you will not have any more control of the situation. While you still need to live in the same place as neighbors, money, time and stress will be spent

Or

You can calm down and start to think what is good for both you. You can take an active role in reaching the right solution that actually is right for both of you with the help of a third party, like mediator, going throw the process but not making the decisions for you.

The first option is called fight in the Court of Law and the second option is called Mediation as alternative method to resolve the same conflict. Both are legitimate methods to resolve conflicts. In the first option everything is out of your own control because someone else will decide for you; in the second option you will have the control of the outcome.

Please take in consideration that in both cases there are money, time and health involved and have consequences.

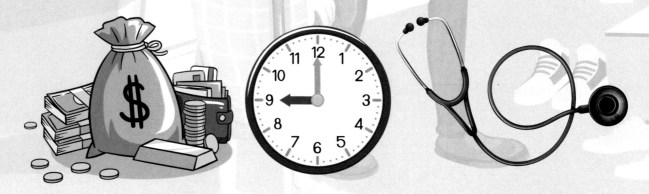

Now take a few minutes to think about what I just said and let me know. I will be waiting upstairs with the other people." Sally says and walks away.

Mr. Gallo and Mrs. Richards are alone in the living room, both are quiet and thinking what Sally just said.

Mr. Gallo says:" *What about sitting down around the table and try to talk and come up with a solution that satisfies everyone taking in consideration all opinions and not make a third party make decisions for us?*

Do you like that idea?

Mrs. Richards was quiet and after few seconds says "*Sure. I would like to sit around the table with you, but with someone that helps us as neutral and impartial party. Let's call Sally as our mediator and see if we can overcome this problem that has been a problem for many months*".

Sally comes down from upstairs to Mrs. Richards and Mr. Gallo. The 3 of them sit around the table in Ben's father work studio.

Sally asks, "*what could be 'the' solution of this problem?*"

"*Well,*" Ben's father starts, "*it has been a family tradition to leave the shoes outside the door, but until today we were living in our own home not in an apartment building.*"

Mrs. Richards is pouting and not

saying anything.

Ben's father says I got an idea: "*what about we put an elegant shoe rack outside our entrance door that will hide in the wall and anytime someone will come into the house we will put the shoes in the rack*".

Sally looks at Mrs. Richards and says:" *it seems to be a great idea, what do you think?*

Mrs. Richard is sitting there, and she doesn't say anything, but her facial expression changed. It seems a little smile came upon her face and her eyes changed from that evil witch to more friendly one.

At this point Sally knew that Mrs. Richards liked the idea and asked to Ben's father:" *Mr. Gallo may I ask you if you have in mind any model and how long will it take to build?*"

Ben's father starts to sketch different types of prototypes on a piece of paper.

Suddenly Mrs. Richards says: "*I like this one!*" pointing to the third sketch on the paper.

Ben's father since he was a young boy loved to draw and went to art school before becoming a diplomat.

At this point Sally asks to both:" *when do you think you can have the shoe rack done?*"

Ben's Father replies:" *I can go to carpenter tomorrow and commission the rack to be done by next week. I will pay for that*".

Mrs. Richards:" *Nodded yes with her head without saying a word*"

Sally says: "*Perfect, I am glad that we could work this out and you both were able to come up with your own solution that is good, easy, everyone is happy, and it does not cost much money.*"

All the guests were upstairs talking and waiting that the mediation to be over. When they see all their faces, Sally, Mr. Gallo and Mrs. Richards, all the guests understood that the problem was solved.

At this point everyone went back downstairs to the food and started eating the amazing food that Ben's Mom prepared. Mrs. Richards even joined the party.

6

Big Waves
"So, What!" When You Know
What To Do You Are Not Afraid!"

6

Big Waves
"So, What!" When You Know
What To Do You Are Not Afraid!"

It's a cold winter afternoon in Southern California.

Despite what they say it's also cold in this beautiful place.

Molly and Jack are in training. It doesn't matter if the air is cold, the water is freezing and there are big waves they need to get in the water to train. If they want to be lifeguards when they grow up, they need to get used to different ocean's conditions. They know very well that they need to train in any kind of conditions to be able to rescue people.

Jack doesn't wear a wetsuit. He is always warm and fearless. Instead, Molly is always cold, doesn't like waves and cold water, but she is the fastest and strongest swimmer in the team. She is cautious and studies the conditions of the ocean very carefully for hours before she gets in.

Jack says:" Come on Molly the water is not super cold today".

Molly replies: "Sure, for you. You are like an Alaskan man and have a physical condition of not feeling cold. Actually, I don't feel my feet for how cold the water is, and I have brain freeze."

Jack laughs and jumps in the water: "I'll wait you at the take-off rock. (take off rock is a rock where you can hide) The water is not so cold and the waves aren't powerful."

"Seriously" Molly says, *"It's obvious, look how big are the waves, and see how much white water from the smashing waves there is. There is no break and the waves are keep coming.,*

"Come on don't be a chicken" Jack screams *"jump in".*

"Ok" Molly replies.

Molly with her wetsuit on, her fins on and goggles, jumps in the freezing water.

Molly and Jack swam under the three big waves. *"We made it out in the open ocean"* Jack says. *"Let's start our swim Molly."*

Sometime passed and Molly says: *"Jack let's go back we are in the water for too long and it's cold"*

"OK" Jack replies.

On the way back they stop just outside the cove to wait for the right time to when there is a break from the waves so they can get back safe. Molly is scared and looks at Jack with a scary look in her face.
"I am scared Jack" Molly says.

Jack replies *"So, What!"*

Molly quietly keeps her eyes on Jack
to wait to get the signal it is ok to go in.

Few minutes pass and
"With a gesture of thumb
up now it's the right time
to go back to the shore"
Jack signals to Molly.

Molly the strongest and fastest
swimmer starts to swim while breathing
only on the right side to check if the waves
are coming. She sprints back to the shore. While
Jack is still in the water few yards back. Molly is back
at the beach and took off her fins and gets on land.

While Jack and Molly were changing Molly asks Jack: " *Jack are you ever afraid of anything?"*

Jack says: "*See Molly we made it safe back to shore. Fears and being afraid are emotions. Becoming hostage of this state of mind can be dangerous. Be trained and cautious is what we are, and I trust my training."*

"If I become hostage of my own fears, I won't be able to think what to do based on what I know. We need to concentrate on what we know and what we know is swimming."

"Never doubt your training and your ability because you are the best swimmer of the team. Never lose your concentration because as soon as you do so, you just put yourself in jeopardy.

You need to rely on your skills, abilities and tools and that makes you able and capable to face any challenges. Beside the fact that you are not alone, you have me and your team whom you can always rely upon. When you are afraid you lose concentration and don't think straight and when you don't think you make mistakes that will always have consequences. "

"We need to work with the waves because like in anything else in life when we are in trouble or in conflicts, we need to hold on what we know to be able to resolve any problems and don't doubt what we know. This is why I say to you "So, what!""

Molly says: "It's like the story the martial arts coach Mr. Jefferson always told us when he trained us"

Jack replies "exactly"

"We need to be a Problem Solver Mr. Jefferson always said" Jack says to Molly.

"Fortunately, there are individuals that know how to manage properly any problems when they arise. We need to be like them. They know how to resolve problems effectively and productively because they focus and rely on what they know.

Those people are called Problem Solvers, and they accept that problems are a "normal" part of life and actually are not afraid of them because they rely on their training. In life when something happens unexpectedly the first reaction is fear because we don't know what to do and what will happen. But instead of being hostage of the fear we need to remember:

"So, what!"

Jack says: "So, what! These two words make you come back into reality and trust your abilities and your team"

Remember what really matters is the attitude towards the conflict, how to see it and how prepared you are dealing with it effectively.

"This is the key." Jack Says.

So, the Problem Solvers think and act to look for the solution that is good for them and they can handle and follow a road map to resolve the problems and act accordingly. Problem Solvers are people trained in using effectively the process to assess the problem together with skills, mind and tools sets to search for "the" right solution and resolve conflict when arises.

"See Molly" Jack says "this is what we did a few minutes ago with the problem of coming back with big waves. We waited for the right time; we trusted our abilities and we acted and swam back"

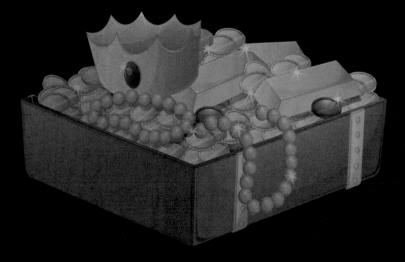

The Red Door And Dark Room.
"Decision-Making Process"

7

The Red Door And Dark Room. "Decision-Making Process"

Jack and Molly grew up spending nights after dinner listening to Sally's stories.

Sally was their babysitter when they were little kids and she was telling the most fascinating stories ever told. The stories were a mix between mystery, scary and mind boggling.

Jack and Molly grew up now and Sally is out to law school.

For years even though Molly and Jack are old now, anytime she is in town she always spends at least one dinner with them.

Few nights ago, they all have dinner in Molly's parents' house.

Jack says, *"Sally, can you tell us one of your stories"*.

Sally starts:

"It is a cold night and a young man is walking around the neighborhood. He cannot sleep so he decides to take a walk. He goes through the park and comes out from the other side and he sees a very unique house. The house has only a red door and no windows."

He gets close to the house to see it closer and suddenly a little old man comes out of nowhere and says:

"Hi, who are you? And what are you doing out so late in a cold night?

The young man replies: "Hi, my name is Bobby and I couldn't sleep. So many thoughts in my head and worries. I took a walk to clear my mind."

The little old man says: *"May I ask what worries you?"*

The young man replies: *"I don't have the ability to know how to make the right decision and knowing when is the right one."*

"Well" the old little man says: *"allow me to share a story."*

behind the red door there is a room. Inside the room there are going to be a pile of gold and also a big hole and the room is pitch dark.

"I am asking you- Do you want to go in?"

What do you answer?

One option is "say yes" — following this decision you can get the gold but also you can fall in the hole and lose everything.

Another option is to says no —following this decision you will never know if you would find the gold or fall in the hole.

Well, if you decide to say yes, let me ask: " how do you think to get in the room?"

The young man is puzzled and doesn't know how to answer.

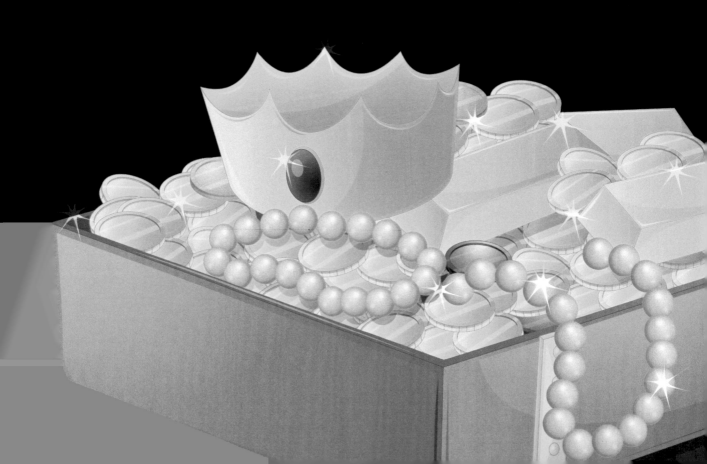

The old little man says:
"When you need to decide
anything, start to think about
all your possibilities from
the craziest and dangerous
to the safest and easy. When
you generate ideas think
outside the box and write them
down on a piece of paper, the right one will come. In spite
of this process you might feel lost in making the decision so you can
reach out for help and share your worries and ideas with others.
The people who you share with is formed by those individuals that
you trust and are next to you that will share their opinions and help
you. Finally, always think and ask yourself:

"What are the consequences?"

"What makes the decision be the right one?"

"Am I able to handle the consequences of my decision?".

Let me tell you my friend: "There is not a universal answer to the
question which is the right decision because each individual is
different and has different upbringing and needs."

"The right decision is right when the consequences are good for
each of us and when each of us are able to handle them without
hurting any other individual."

All of us perceive reality in a different way. We are happy
and satisfied with different things in our lives therefore
each individual needs to learn how to be effective in the
decision-making process to resolve each problem or issue
effectively and productively for themselves. One of the
biggest mistakes that most people run into is that they make
decisions based on past experiences. Another big mistake
is not making ANY decision.

At the end the little old man says: "*The best answer is slowly inching your foot with your hand on the wall until you will find the switch to turn the light on and see where the gold is and where the hole might be*". "*Life is the pitch-black room you need to find the switch to recognize the risk and reward*".

To be able to find a switch: you need to gather information; not assume to know what other people think; listen to others and learn from them and find your own path; find your team of people to help you when you need them — that means understand how important is the "power of association" who you associate with. Whoever you do associate with can keep you down or keep where you are and cause failure or help you to elevate yourselves and achieve success.

Be humble — Don't brag about the good things you do or have,, one day you will understand and appreciate.

Be respectful and honest — your reputation will speak for you.

Take full responsibility of your actions.

The young man is puzzled by the story and is glad he met the "little old man". He gets home and writes down everything the little old man said to be able to process the information and never forget. Next time to know how to make a right decision.

Jack and Molly say:" *this time, Sally, the story is the most amazing story you ever told us.*"

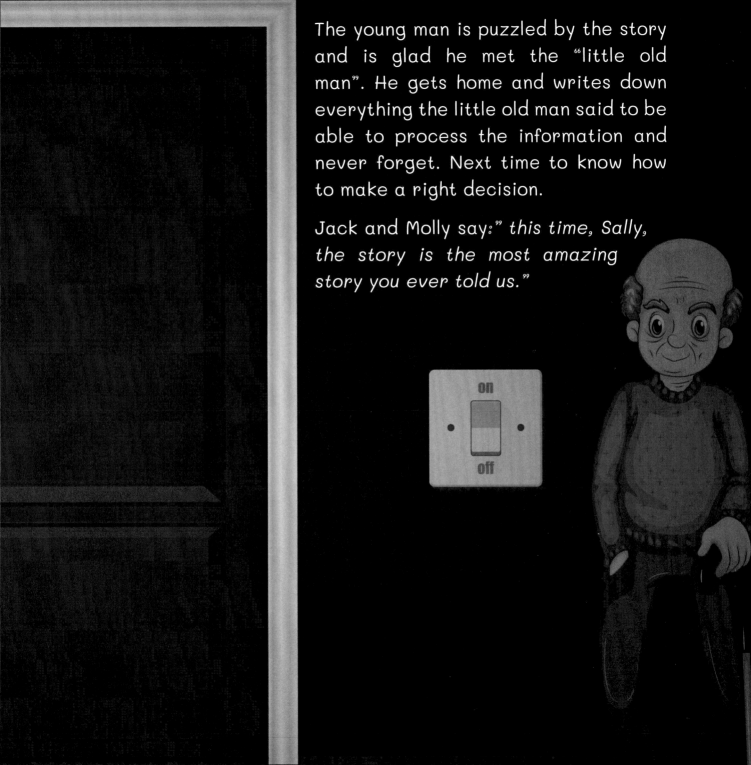

Happy Playground
"The" Solution

8

Happy Playground
"The" Solution

Molly and Jack slept in today.

Today they are going to meet Sally to share with her what they learned from all the adventures and experiences of the week.

They walk to the park close to their homes where Sally is waiting for them. She is sitting on a bench under a big tree in the shade to protect herself from the sun.

While they are still walking toward the park Molly says:

"Jack, do you agree that we are conflict free. When life will throw difficult situations at us, I am confident we have the skill to know what to do and how to deal with them. I believe we are skilled not to be afraid of conflicts."

Jack replies: *"Yes, I think so."*

Molly says to Jack: *"Do you know why we are not afraid of conflicts?"*

Jack replies: *"I think we are not afraid of them because we know what conflict is and how to act on it. We understood the conflict won't resolve itself. We always need to work to find 'the' right solution for us and to build a happy life."*

Jack and Molly arrive at the park where Sally was waiting. Both of them ask her: "*Sally it's so nice seeing you. Sally we have a question for you: why when adults are involved in conflict or in any kind of problem or difficult situation, they struggle in making the right decision to reach 'the' right solution?*"

Sally smiles and with a warm and soft tone of voice says:

"*Molly, Jack come in the shade.*

Let me explain something very important that you need to understand when you apply the problem-solving process. When you get at the end of the problem-solving process and you need to decide which solution will resolve the conflict. There is a big difference between "A" solution and "THE" solution."

"A" solution is general and based on principles. Generally, it's made by a third party that doesn't know the real reasons of why the conflict arises. "A" solution doesn't actually end the conflict because is made on principles instead of on what is good for the parties, what they want, and what they can handle.

"THE" solution, on the other hand, is made essentially by the parties involved in the conflict. Often, they can ask for the help and guidance of a third person that will keep impartial and neutral in helping them search for "the" right solution for them.

"The" right solution is right when it's realistic, doable, satisfactory, and cost effective and it is made in a reasonable time. Sally says

Molly and Jack ask Sally: "

What does realistic mean?

What does doable mean?"

What does satisfactory mean?

What does cost effective mean?

What does time sensitive mean? "

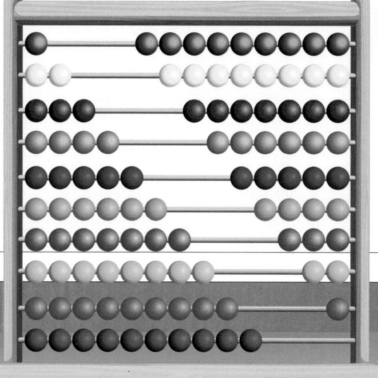

Sally replies to them:

"Well, realistic means that it's good, practical and can be achieved in real life.

Doable means what the person needs to do is practicable, possible to realize.

Satisfactory means the things that need to be done will make people happy.

Cost effective means that the process to achieve the solution won't cost so much money and the person can afford it.

Time sensitive means that the solution needs to be done in a short time. Often when a lot time passes by, things don't have the same meaning.

When you are choosing the right solution, if you are involved in the problem you need to keep in mind that eventually you need to give up something. When you give up something you need to know what you can leave with and without.

Sally smiles and asks Molly and Jack:

"Do you *think you are going to be able to recognize 'the' solution from 'a' solution?*"

The kids look at each other and reply: "Now after your explanation we have a check list to follow to search for "the" right solution and move forward.

Sally says:

"*Very good kids. Following the roadmap and the decision-making process to reach "the" right solution rather than "a" solution is what will end the conflict.*

Molly asks: "What happens if I don't follow the decision-making process?"

Sally looks at the kids and with a warm voice says:

"*If and when the decision-making process is not applied correctly, it can bring you into the wrong decision and consequently a miserable life because one thing is true: everyone needs to leave with "the" solution. So, better it is the right one. Do you agree?*"

Jack and Molly are paying attention to what Sally is saying and remember all the adventures they experienced.

Jack says: "*Sally can you tell us again about the decision-making process to get to "the" right solution.*"

Sally smiles and hugs the kids and says:

"*Let's start with something people don't like to hear. All of us are responsible of our actions, what we say, how we want to feel and how we spend our time.*"

Remember kids Sally says:

"*We cannot change others, but we can change ourselves and we need to be responsible for what we say, do and how we spend time.*

In life there are positive and negative events on which we do not have any control at all, and we cannot do anything about it. Some of these events are bad and not pleasant.

If we follow the decision-making process will leads us to "the" solution that is right for us and we can live with it.

To be sure "the" solution is the right one and we can live with ask to yourself the following questions:

"Can we change the events when they already happened?"

When you try to answer this question remember to keep in mind life is made out of many events. Some of the events can be prevented, some of them depend on our actions or what we say, and some others are out of our control.

We need to be able to recognize the three different scenarios.

If the event depends on our actions or what we say, we should think and ask ourselves if we are able to handle the consequences and if you realize it's your responsibility say "sorry".

Here something that can help you: I suggest to both of you talk less and listen more because when you listen to what others are saying you learn and able to gather information. When you have the right information, you are able to reach "the" right solution and most important you don't assume to know what people think.

If the events are out of our control when they happened, the only thing we can do is control how we will react to them.

The reaction and the decision that we are going to make after the event will depend fully on us. The decision can make us happy or miserable.

For example, think kids what happens if when you wake up in the morning you don't know what to wear. The red t-shirt or the blue t-shirt or even the one with Superman on it. What do you do?

You go to your mom and ask her opinion, after that you go to your sister and ask her opinion and finally you go to your dad to ask his opinion. Let's say that all the three of them will have three different opinions. What do you do?

At the end you will choose the color that you like the most.

At the end of the day you are the one that will make the final decision.

There is not a universal "right" decision or solution because each individual is different and like different things.

We will know it is the right decision for us when we are going through the process and we are able to handle the consequences and make us happy.

Molly jumps in the conversation and says:

"For what I understood to be able to make the right decision we need to understand several concepts:

We need to be able to let go. That means we cannot live in the past. The past experiences cannot come back and cannot change.

We cannot live life thinking that our happiness is in something that we don't have or in the hand of someone else.

Finally, we need to know ourselves."

Sally says: "Excellent!"

Jack says: "How do you know when you are happy with the decision?"

Sally says: "For sure remember you cannot be happy with what you don't have instead you need to be happy with what you have. Is that correct?

People are all different and perceive reality in different ways so we can only search for what makes us happy and not happy and respect the other people decisions.

When we don't like something, we can decide to be sad and mad or focus to change and improve the situation.

Jack and Molly, they get up and thank Sally and start running in the playground.

Jerry The Rooster
The "After" Conflict

9

Jerry The Rooster
The "After" Conflict

Molly and Jack met Sally and asked her:

"What happens "After" you find "the" solution to the conflict?"

Sally says: *"See kids, here's the big secret. The end point of any problem-solving process is not "the" solution but what happen after you find the solution.*

In the Happy Playground story, we talked about "the" solution, now let me explain to you why it's so important the "After" conflict."

As we said "the" solution is not the end of the problem-solving process in fact, how you handle the "After" conflict is important as well.

The "After" conflict means, what will happen after you find the solution to the problem. If you are able to deal with the "After" conflict in the right way it allows you to live a happy life.

The wrong solution and the inability to manage post-conflict will determine the continuation of the conflict.

To be able to handle correctly the "After" conflict you must keep in mind a few things. Every time you are involved in a conflict the reality you are used to will change. In order to resolve the conflict and move forward you need to manage the new reality that has been created. To do so take the time needed to adjust to the "After" conflict which means act and accept the new reality.

This will allow you to say that the conflict is over.

When a problem happens, we can do two things: you can worry and don't do anything just be frustrated or you can act to try to resolve the problem and find "the" solution and live with it.

To be able to choose the second option each of us needs to let go the past. Never keep your negative emotions inside such as revenge, madness and resentment but focus on positive emotions and do the best you can to change what you don't like.

Keep in mind its always your choice on what you want to do.

The biggest mistake you can do is to blame others for what we don't have or don't like.

Molly and Jack ask:" *Sally, do you have a new story before we go home that explains the "After" conflicts?*"

122

"OK kids here's the last story that will make you understand how important is to think and take in consideration the "After" conflict Sally replies "and after we, all will go home."

Susan and Peter live in a countryside.

Every morning Peter wakes up early and gets ready to start his day. He gets out of the house and stops first in the chicken coop to get the eggs and then in the barn to milk the cows.

He brings some of the eggs and the milk back in the house for Susan's breakfast and the rest he will bring later on to the market in the city.

Today, is a rainy and gloomy morning and Peter wears boots and a rain jacket and walks to the chicken coop and barn. While he is walking, he sees Jerry the rooster with his back on the ground and his legs up in the air complaining.

"AUCHHH ohhh my back hurts", Jerry says

Peter runs towards Jerry the rooster and hears him saying: "why has this happened to me today?".

Peter gets close to Jerry the rooster and says: "What happened Jerry?"

Jerry replies: "why did this happen to me today?"

Peter says: "Jerry don't reply to my question with another question?

I don't have the answer of why things happened in the way they happen, and I can tell you: every time a tumble happens is normal to ask why me and get mad, sad and cry but unfortunately there is no answer to this question and that emotions won't help.

Sooner or later you need to get up and get back on your own two legs.

Instead of spending time asking: "why me? Think of your responsibilities."

You have many responsibilities: you need to take care of all the chickens in the coop and make sure that they will be happy to make fresh eggs; you need to sing at sunrise to wake up the village. Even I rely on you to wake me up. I also rely on you to always have fresh eggs from happy chickens so I can sell them and take care of you and the other chickens."

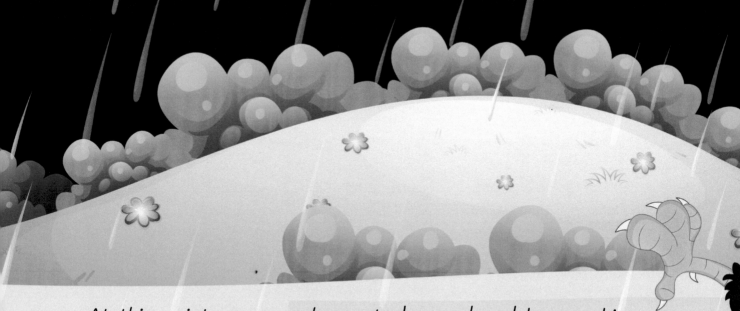

At this point you can choose to be mad and keep asking "why me", and stay with your legs up in the air and not do anything or choose to find the way somehow to stand back up.

Each of us need to choose to stand up or stay down with legs up, cry and complain why me and repeat to ourselves "this time it's too hard to stand up so I will stay here".

The truth is that at the end of the day each of us will find the strength to stand up. All of us are different and have different times and ways to get back on our feet.

Some people with a quick leap are back on their own feet; others stay on one side and kneel to stand up; others strugle a lot until somehow, they are back on their feet all sweaty and out of breath.

When we are back on our feet it seems, we don't remember how we got on the floor and more important we don't remember the main question: "why me?"

What we focus on is that now we are back on our feet and we are happy to be standing and we start to see things in different ways, and even we see new things. We change our way of viewing things like we have special glasses and we feel the feeling the joy of being back to our responsibilities with a different mind set.

This feeling of joy is what we need to remember for the next time that we will fall, and our legs are going up in the air and the world seems upside down. We need to remember the things that make us happy such as small things, the things that make us who we are and our responsibilities.

Jerry the roster decides to stand up on his legs. He has too many responsibilities and he loves all of them. He likes to be to rooster.

Sally smiles and says to Molly and Jack:
"let's go home and treasure the stories
you have lived and learned".

Few minutes later Sally adds: *"Before you go home here some tools for both of you to keep in mind and something to remember.*

Ask yourself:

"Why do I want to give my precious time to something I don't like or someone that doesn't want to be with me?

When you answering the question remember to start focusing on the positive. Time is the only thing that we cannot buy and is limited so why give it to something that is not good for us.

It's our responsibility to decide how we want to feel and what we want to do.

We are responsible for our actions, what we say and how we say it.

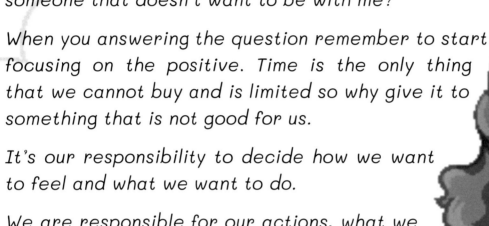

It's always wise to choose to be quiet when you don't know what to say. When you don't talk you can listen, if you listen, you can learn, and if you learn you will be able to make the right decision to reach the right solution.

We don't have the control on external events or actions of others, but we are responsible on how we react to them.

Remember actions and words have meaning and they can be as harmful weapons and they determinate the success or failure of the interaction with other people.

PROBLEM-SOLVING ROAD MAP TO ANY TYPE OF CONFLICT EFFECTIVELY

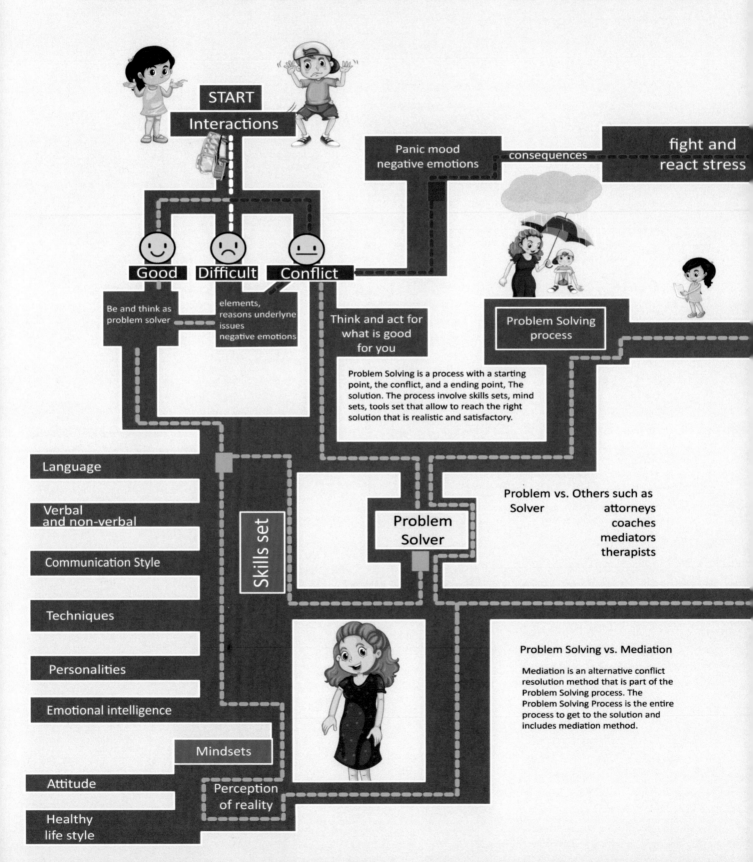

START
Interactions

Panic mood negative emotions — consequences — fight and react stress

Good   Difficult   Conflict

Be and think as problem solver

elements, reasons underlyne issues negative emotions

Think and act for what is good for you

Problem Solving process

Problem Solving is a process with a starting point, the conflict, and a ending point, The solution. The process involve skills sets, mind sets, tools set that allow to reach the right solution that is realistic and satisfactory.

Language

Verbal and non-verbal

Communication Style

Skills set

Problem vs. Others such as
Solver   attorneys
               coaches
               mediators
               therapists

Problem Solver

Techniques

Personalities

Emotional intelligence

Problem Solving vs. Mediation

Mediation is an alternative conflict resolution method that is part of the Problem Solving process. The Problem Solving Process is the entire process to get to the solution and includes mediation method.

Mindsets

Attitude   Perception of reality

Healthy life style

RESOLVE
AND PRODUCTIVELY

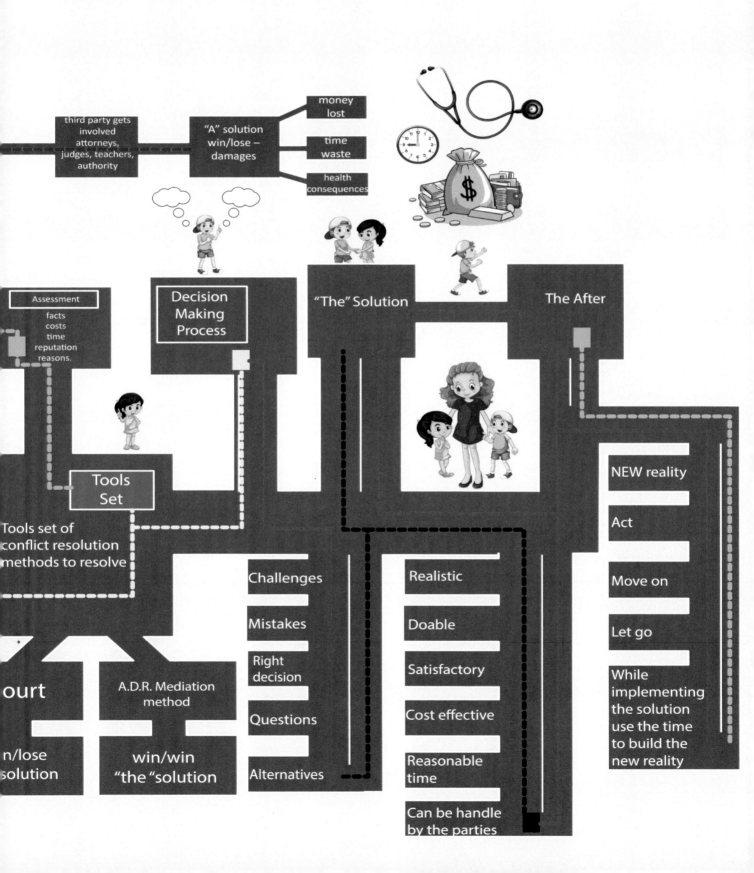